This book belongs to:

....

Based on the episode "Paddington and the Three Musketeers" by Michelle Membu-Philip

Adapted by Rebecca Gerlings

First published in the United Kingdom by HarperCollins *Children's Books* in 2024
HarperCollins *Children's Books* is a division of HarperCollins*Publishers* Ltd
1 London Bridge Street
London SE1 9GF

www.harpercollins.co.uk

HarperCollins*Publishers*
Macken House, 39/40 Mayor Street Upper
Dublin 1, D01 C9W8, Ireland

1 3 5 7 9 10 8 6 4 2

ISBN: 978-0-00-862159-9

Printed in Malaysia

The Adventures of Paddington™

The Book Day Quest

HarperCollins *Children's Books*

Dear Aunt Lucy,

This week, we've had so much fun celebrating Book Day in Windsor Gardens. We all dressed up as our favourite book characters. There was even a prize for the best costume . . .

It was Book Day and Jonathan was very excited about the prize for the best costume.

"The Megabike 300! Isn't it awesome, Paddington?" he exclaimed, waving the picture at him.

"It is!" replied Paddington. "But today I'm *not* just Paddington – I'm . . . Musketeer Paddington!"

"Well, we're Hansel and Gretel," said Jonathan. "It's a story about a brother and sister who live in an enchanted forest and find a gingerbread house."

Paddington thought their costumes were wonderful, especially the baskets of sweets.

"Hi, guys!" Mateo called, climbing into the treehouse. **"Wow!** You all look amazing for Book Day!"

"You too, Mateo," replied Paddington. "You look so . . . *effortless.* Which book character are you?"

"Oh, I–I'm not dressed up," replied Mateo. "I–I don't have a favourite book."

"But if you don't wear a costume you won't have a chance of **winning the prize,**" Judy pointed out.

Mateo looked at the picture of the Megabike 300 and sighed.

"It would be **amazing** to win it, but I haven't enjoyed reading since I was little," he explained. "I couldn't dress up as just *any* book character."

"But books and reading are *wonderful,* Mateo!" said Paddington.
"Once I start, I can't stop!"

WHOOSH!

"It's great you love to read," said Mateo sadly. "I wish I still did. But it's too late – I'll never find a book and a costume in time."

"All it takes is one book . . ." said Paddington, thinking hard.

"I know!" he exclaimed. "We can go to Mr Gruber's shop! He's mending my favourite book, *The Three Musketeers*. We can find a book you'll love there – and a character for you to dress up as!"

In the kitchen, Paddington and the children bumped into Mrs Brown and Mrs Bird.

"Oh, you look great, Musketeer Paddington!" said Mrs Brown. "I'm the Mad Hatter from *Alice in Wonderland*!"

"Thank you, but I think the tea has turned Mrs Bird's face green," whispered Paddington, looking worried.

"It's not the tea!" said Mrs Bird, cackling. "I'm the Wicked Witch of the West!"

Suddenly Mr Brown burst in. "Where's my magnifying glass for my **Sherlock Holmes** costume?" he cried, hunting through the kitchen drawers.

"Couldn't you use the one in your pocket?" Paddington suggested.

"Aha!" exclaimed Mr Brown, holding it up triumphantly. "The game is afoot!"

At the front door, Paddington came face to face with a pirate.

"Toq?" asked Paddington.

"It's Long John Silver!" declared the pirate.

"Oh! Your favourite book must be *Treasure Island*!" said Jonathan.

"Aye! And ye won't believe what I found at me doorstep today . . ."

Toq pulled a scrap of paper from her pocket. "THIS!"

"The black spot!" gasped Judy.

"What *is* the black spot?" asked Paddington.

"It means ye've been marked and if ye found guilty, ye walk the plank," Toq explained.

"Arghhh!" they all cried, picturing having to walk the plank surrounded by hungry sharks.

Mr Curry appeared, dressed as Sherlock Holmes, demanding to know what all the noise was about.

"Toq's got *the black spot*!" replied Paddington.

"Looks like a big ink splot to me," Mr Curry snapped. Seeing their disappointed faces, he peered at it again. "Ahem . . . now I've had a closer look this could very well be *the* real black spot."

"Cool! To Book Day!" shouted Judy, Jonathan and Toq as they skipped away, and Mateo and Paddington headed to Mr Gruber's shop.

"By the way, nice Mr Brown costume, Mr Curry!" Paddington called back.

"W-w-whaaaat!?" exclaimed Mr Curry. Just then Mr Brown came out, and Mr Curry saw his costume – they were identical!

"Ahhh, Musketeer Paddington!" Mr Gruber said as Paddington and Mateo walked into his shop. "Your book is repaired and ready to read!"

"I can't wait to read it again. Thank you, Mr Gruber!" said Paddington, hugging *The Three Musketeers* to his chest.

"I am **Peter Pan** today, Paddington!" said Mr Gruber.

"Well, Peter Pan, Mateo would like to find a book that he loves so he can find a character to dress up as too."

"You've come to the right place!" said Mr Gruber.

A short while later, Judy, Jonathan and Toq arrived at the town hall.

Jonathan gasped at the prize. "The Megabike 300! It's *even better* than the picture!"

"Not long now until the winner of the best costume is announced," said Ms Potts.

Judy and Toq exchanged worried glances.

"I really hope Paddington and Mateo make it back in time," said Judy.

"And your dad and Mr Curry," added Mrs Brown.

Where *was* everybody?

Back at Mr Gruber's shop, Mateo still hadn't found the right book.

"Oh, I'll never find a favourite character to dress up as," he said glumly. "I just have to accept that **I'm not going to win.**"

"We'll find a book you love, Mateo," said Paddington.

Just then he had an idea. "Would you like to read *The Three Musketeers*? It's a story about **friendship** and **being a hero!**" he said, handing Mateo his book.

It opened on a page showing an epic sword fight. Paddington told Mateo all about how D'Artagnan met Athos, Porthos and Aramis — **the bravest swordsmen in France** — and together they defeated the evil Cardinal Richelieu!

At last, Mateo had found a favourite book – and a character to dress up as. "I love it!" said Mateo. "I can't wait to read it again and again! Thank you, Paddington. We make a great team!"

"Just like the musketeers," replied Paddington. "All for one . . ."

". . . And one for all!" declared Paddington and Mateo, just as Mr Brown and Mr Curry ran into them – *OOF!* – and went flying.

"Ow!" they both cried, landing in a heap.

"We're both Sherlock Holmes," Mr Curry explained. "But there's only ONE Sherlock!"

"So now we've got *no* chance of winning that bike," said Mr Brown sadly.

"I've got an idea!" said Mateo. "Do you both like *The Three Musketeers*?"

Mr Brown and Mr Curry nodded.

"Then . . . let's all go as them!" he suggested.

"Wonderful idea, Mateo!" agreed Paddington. "Even though the book is called *The Three Musketeers*, by the end there are four of them. Just like there are four of us!"

Their idea certainly seemed to impress the judges. And the amazing sword fighting sealed the deal.

"The winners of the best Book Day costume are . . . the Four Musketeers!" Ms Potts announced.

They'd done it! The audience clapped and whooped for joy.

"All for one . . ." said the Four Musketeers together ". . . and one for all!"

Although it was lovely to win the Megabike 300 with my fellow musketeers, in the end, Aunt Lucy, what made Book Day so special was helping Mateo find his love of reading again.

Love from,
Paddington